3

Who's Coming Tonight?

Written by Jeong-im Choi

Illustrated by Min-jeong Gahng

Edited by Joy Cowley

Autumn came to the little lake.
The ducks were swimming
and the leaves were falling.
All was peaceful and calm.

2

Then, one day, a wild goose flew in.
"Be careful!" the goose warned.
"An evil red fox is in the forest."

The ducks quacked with fear.
Would the evil red fox eat them?

They saw a letter on a leaf,
tacked to the bark of a tree.
That letter made their feathers
stand on end.

I'm coming
tonight!
Red Fox

The ducks had a meeting
and made a plan.
"We can't all stay awake.
We need three sentries
who will wake us up
when the fox appears."

So three young strong ducks
were chosen to stay awake
all night, on sentry duty.

Night fell and the lake was dark.
The three sentries said,
"We will guard the lake
without blinking our eyes,
without nodding off."

That's how they stood all night,
their eyes wide open.
But the evil red fox
did not come that night.

The next night,
the three ducks guarded the lake.
They blinked their eyes
and nodded off.
The fox did not come.

On the third night,
the ducks were so tired
they went to a swamp and slept.

When they woke up
and went back to the lake,
it was empty!
The fox had been there!

The ducks were upset. They quacked,
"This happened because we neglected
our sentry duty. We need a plan
to rescue all our friends
from the evil red fox."

They put their heads together.
Then they wrote on a leaf:
We're coming tonight!
Three Ducks

When the red fox saw the note,
he sneered. "Silly ducks!
They are copying my trick!
I'll catch them and eat them all!"

Night fell, and the red fox waited,
not moving an inch,
for the three ducks.

The next night, the red fox
did not blink his eyes
nor did he nod off.

18

On the third night,
he still kept his eyes wide open.

On the fourth morning,
his bloodshot eyes closed.
"I have to get some sleep
to get ready for tonight,"
he mumbled.

19

Snore, snore, snore.

While the fox's snores
echoed through the forest,
the three ducks rescued
all the ducks in the fox's net.

20

Then they cast the net
over the sleeping fox.

Some wild geese flying south
picked up the fox in the net.
They would take him far away
from the forest.

22

Thanks to the three ducks,
the evil red fox was gone.
The ducks swam on the lake.
The autumn leaves fell.
All was peaceful and calm again.

25

Dear Three Brave Ducks,

Thank you for saving us from the evil red fox.
You tried to guard us every night, and we understand
that you got tired when the red fox did not show up.
However, when the fox took us all, you came to save us.
Although there was great danger, you acted in a responsible way.
You are the brave peacekeepers of our beautiful lake.

From the grateful ducks

big & SMALL

Original Korean text by Jeong-im Choi
Illustrations by Min-jeong Gahng
Original Korean edition © Eenbook

This English edition published by big & SMALL
by arrangement with Eenbook
English text edited by Joy Cowley
Additional editing by Mary Lindeen
Artwork for this edition produced
in cooperation with Norwood House Press, U.S.A.
English edition © big & SMALL 2015

ISBN: 978-1-925233-94-0

Printed in Korea